Shake Your Tail Feathers

Adapted by Andrea Posner-Sanchez
from the script "Professor Pancake" by Kent Redeker

Based on the television series created by Chris Nee

Illustrated by Mike Wall

 A GOLDEN BOOK · NEW YORK

ISBN 978-0-7364-3274-0 (trade) — ISBN 978-0-7364-3300-6 (ebook)
Printed in the United States of America
10 9 8 7 6 5 4 3 2 1

One night, Doc McStuffins and her toys are pretending to roast marshmallows over a campfire. "I hope I don't burn my mouth," says Chilly. "That's not a real fire," Lambie points out.

"And those aren't even marshmallows,"
adds Doc. "They're cotton balls."

"Well, if we can't eat them, what should
we do with them?" Chilly asks.

Stuffy has an idea. The dragon grabs a cotton ball in each hand. He tosses one at Doc and one at Chilly and yells, "Cotton ball fight!"

Everyone joins in. Soon the room is covered in a blizzard of cotton balls.

"That was fun!" says Doc. "But now it's time for bed."

Lambie and Doc enjoy a quiet cuddle as Bronty the dinosaur leaps around the room shouting, "I'm not sleepy, Doc. See! See! Not sleepy!"

Doc decides a story will help Bronty settle down.
"And there's nobody better at reading bedtime stories
than Professor Hootsburgh."

Doc goes to the bookshelf to get her toy owl. But
the owl isn't there. "Professor Hootsburgh! Where are
you?" she calls.

The toys begin to search the room for Professor Hootsburgh.

"There's something sticking out from under the toy box!" Bronty cries.

Doc rushes over and lifts one side of the toy box.
"Brave dragon going in!" Stuffy announces as he dives
under the box—and pulls out Professor Hootsburgh.

Doc uses her magic stethoscope to bring the toy owl to life. Professor Hootsburgh is all flat and floppy. The owl explains that she fell off her shelf when Doc was cleaning the room a few days ago. "And you must not have seen me, because you set the toy box on top of me," Professor Hootsburgh recalls.

Doc feels awful. "I would have rescued you right away if I knew you were down there!" she exclaims.

"Oh, I know that, Doc," Professor Hootsburgh says. "You always help toys!"

Doc wants to give Professor Hootsburgh a checkup, but the professor insists on reading everyone a bedtime story first. So Doc and the toys gather around the toy box, ready to listen to one of their favorite stories.

But the professor is too weak to hold herself up.

She soon topples over!

"Please, Professor," says Doc. "If you let me give you a checkup, we can figure out the best way to help you."

Lambie gives the owl a hug. "And if you're scared, we'll all be there for you."

Professor Hootsburgh agrees. Hallie brings over Doc's doctor bag.

Doc listens to Professor Hootsburgh's heart with her stethoscope.

Then Doc checks Professor Hootsburgh's blood pressure.

"I have a diagnosis!" Doc exclaims. "You have a case of squished-flatatosis."

The professor looks concerned until Doc explains that all she has to do to feel better is get back in shape. "And the best way to do that is to get up and get moving!"

"You can shake your tail feathers!" suggests Stuffy. Then he and Bronty leap up and shake their tails to show Professor Hootsburgh how.

Doc turns on some music to get everyone moving.
Professor Hootsburgh needs help at first, but soon
she's hooting and dancing and having a great time.

The professor's stuffing settles into all the right spots. "Oh, my goodness me! I am officially back in shape!" she shouts. "I'm going to make getting up and moving a part of my daily life from now on."

The dance party is over and it is time, once again, for bed. Everyone snuggles together as Professor Hootsburgh starts to read. Before long, the toys are snoring.

Doc picks up Professor Hootsburgh for a good-night hug. "Looks like your bedtime story did the trick," she says to her owl friend.

"Well, I *am* an expert at bedtime stories, just like you're an expert at fixing toys."